Powerful Predators

Lisa M. Herrington

Content Consultants

Becky Ellsworth
Curator of Shores Region

Nikki Smith
Assistant Curator of North America
and Polar Frontier Regions
Columbus Zoo and Aquarium,
Columbus, Ohio

Reading Consultant

Jeanne M. Clidas, Ph.D.
Reading Specialist

Children's Press®
An Imprint of Scholastic Inc.

Library of Congress Cataloging-in-Publication Data
Names: Herrington, Lisa M., author.
Title: Powerful predators: Sharks! Polar Bears! Lions!/by Lisa M. Herrington.
Description: New York, NY: Children's Press, 2018. | Series: Rookie star.
Extraordinary animals | Includes index.
Identifiers: LCCN 2017025797 | ISBN 9780531230916 (library binding) | ISBN 9780531233801 (pbk)
Subjects: LCSH: Predatory animals—Juvenile literature.
Classification: LCC QL758 .H47 2018 | DDC 591.5/3—dc23
LC record available at https://lccn.loc.gov/2017025797

Produced by Spooky Cheetah Press
Art direction: Keith Plechaty for kwpCreative
Creative direction: Judith E. Christ for Scholastic
Art direction: Brenda Jackson for Scholastic

Published in 2019 by Children's Press, an imprint of Scholastic Inc.

Printed in Johor Bahru, Malaysia 108

SCHOLASTIC, CHILDREN'S PRESS, ROOKIE STAR™, and associated logos are trademarks and/or registered trademarks of Scholastic Inc.

1 2 3 4 5 6 7 8 9 10 R 28 27 26 25 24 23 22 21 20 19

Scholastic Inc., 557 Broadway, New York, NY 10012.

Photographs ©: cover: Tierfotoagentur/m.blue-shadow/age fotostock; 1: Chris and Monique Fallows/NPL/Minden Pictures; 2: Tony Wu/Nature Picture Library; 3: Chris & Monique Fallows/Nature Picture Library; 4-5: Tony Crocetta/Getty Images; 6-7: George Grall/Getty Images; 8-9: JUNIORS BILDARCHIV/age fotostock; 9 inset: Rhinie van Meurs/NiS/Minden Pictures; 10 inset: Henrik Sorensen/Getty Images; 10-11: Fred Bruemmer/Getty Images; 12 inset: Will Burrard-Lucas/Nature Picture Library; 12-13: kiwisoul/iStockphoto; 14-15: Alan Murphy/BIA/Minden Pictures; 15 inset: kojihirano/Getty Images; 16-17: Shem Compion/FLPA/Minden Pictures; 17 inset: Mark Stevenson/Stocktrek Images/Getty Images; 18-19: Aditya "Dicky" Singh/Alamy Images; 19 inset: Sandesh Kadur/NPL/Minden Pictures; 20 inset: Denis Scott/Getty Images; 20-21: Alessandro De Maddalena/Shutterstock; 22 inset: Eric Baccega//NPL/Minden Pictures; 22-23: Fuse/Getty Images; 24-25: Piotr Naskrecki/Minden Pictures; 25 inset: James H Robinson/Getty Images; 26 inset: Yoshiharu Sekino/Science Source; 26-27: Yashpal Rathore/NPL/Minden Pictures; 28 top: Daniela Dirscherl/Getty Images; 28-29 ribbons: _human/iStockphoto; 29 top: Kim Taylor/NPL/Minden Pictures; 30 top left: Pcha988/iStockphoto; 30 center left: Tom Murphy/Getty Images; 30 bottom left: D. Parer & E. Parer-Cook/Minden Pictures/Superstock, Inc.; 30 top right: Geoff Dann/Getty Images; 30 center right: Adam Gault/Media Bakery; 30 bottom right: Eureka/Alamy Images; 31 bottom: Piotr Naskrecki/Minden Pictures; 31 top: Rhinie van Meurs/NiS/Minden Pictures; 31 center top: Tony Crocetta/Getty Images; 31 center bottom: Shem Compion/FLPA/Minden Pictures; 32: Mark J. Thomas/Getty Images.

Table of Contents

What Is a Predator?

A **predator** is an animal that kills other animals for food. The African lion is one of the fiercest predators on the planet. No animal wants to face this big cat! Lions hunt in groups called prides. They can take down large **prey** like zebras and buffalo.

Lions have knifelike teeth, razor-sharp claws, and powerful muscles.

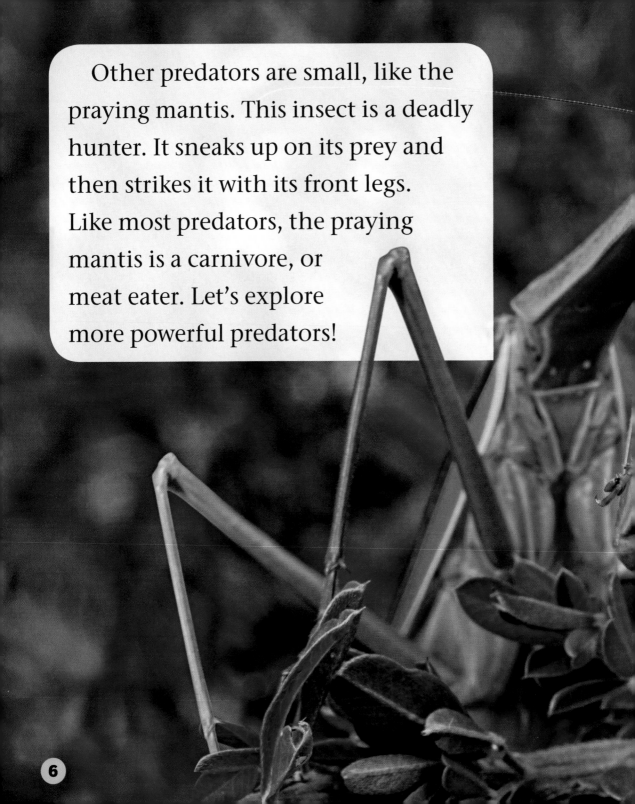

Other predators are small, like the praying mantis. This insect is a deadly hunter. It sneaks up on its prey and then strikes it with its front legs. Like most predators, the praying mantis is a carnivore, or meat eater. Let's explore more powerful predators!

praying mantis

grasshopper

A praying mantis grips a grasshopper in its front legs. Then...*Chomp*!

Chapter 1

Top Predators

The fiercest animals sit on top of their **food chain**. They have no enemies. The orca, or killer whale, is one of the ocean's deadliest hunters. It can grow as big as a school bus. Despite its size, a killer whale can leap out of the water to catch food. The huge hunter can even throw its body onto shore to grab a sea lion.

Orcas, or killer whales, are not whales. They are actually the largest member of the dolphin family.

It is easy to see why orcas are called killer whales. They target everything—seals, fish, turtles, and even sharks and whales. Orcas can make waves strong enough to knock seals off floating ice and into the water.

Mighty polar bears rule the icy Arctic, where they hunt their favorite food—seals. They are the biggest meat eaters on land. A polar bear waits near a hole in the ice. When a seal pops up for air, the hungry bear pounces. In one sitting, a polar bear can eat enough meat to equal 400 hamburgers!

Polar bears are incredible swimmers. In fact, they are even called sea bears. Polar bears paddle with their front paws. Sometimes they swim long distances in search of food.

Super sniffer: A polar bear can smell a seal from miles away.

This huge dragon does not breathe fire. But it is deadly. Komodo dragons are actually lizards. They use their sawlike teeth and long claws to attack prey. A Komodo can even knock a deer to the ground with its powerful tail.

Komodo dragons live in Indonesia. They have an appetite for nearly any animal— dead or alive. These massive lizards flick their forked tongues to smell food miles away.

Komodo dragons are the world's largest and heaviest lizards. They are usually as long as a small car.

The bald eagle is the national bird of the United States.

14

You may not think of birds as fierce. But the bald eagle is one of the sky's top predators. It uses its excellent eyesight to hunt. From high in the sky, a bald eagle spots its prey in the water below. It swoops down and uses its sharp claws to grab the fish. Then the eagle uses its curved beak to rip its meal apart.

The great horned owl is another bird that hunts. It uses its super vision to hunt at night. A great horned owl can swivel its head in any direction. Soft feathers let it fly silently. Rabbits, snakes, and skunks never even hear the owl coming.

Chapter 2

Ambush Hunters

Many dangerous animals ambush their prey. They stay hidden and then strike without warning. A crocodile floats quietly along with just its eyes and nose above the surface of the water. When an antelope stops for a drink, the crocodile strikes. It drags its victim under to drown it.

crocodile

Crocodiles have roamed the Earth since dinosaurs lived. That is when one of the most fearsome predators of all time ruled the land. *T. rex* was among the largest meat-eating dinosaurs on the planet. *T. rex* had teeth the length of your 12-inch (30-centimeter) ruler!

A Nile crocodile hunts wildebeests as they cross a river in Africa.

At about 600 pounds (272 kilograms), a tiger is the world's largest cat. Yet this massive powerhouse can silently stalk its prey. In a flash, the tiger leaps onto an unsuspecting deer (pictured). Then it kills the animal with a bite to the neck.

Tigers usually hunt alone.

Can you spot the tiger?
It is hiding in the tall grass.
Many predators use
camouflage to sneak up on
prey. Their colors or patterns
blend in with the surrounding
area so that they cannot be
seen. No two tigers have the
same stripe pattern.

The great white shark is as terrifying as it looks. It is the largest meat-eating fish in the ocean. From below, the shark searches for seals at the surface. With a burst of speed, it explodes out of the water and grabs a seal in its deadly jaws.

Chomp! **The great white has** rows of razor-sharp teeth. If the shark loses a tooth, a new one moves forward to replace it.

Great whites can detect a small amount of blood in the water from up to 3 miles (5 kilometers) away.

Chapter 3

Extreme Killers

Do you see the hump on this grizzly's back? The bears get their power and strength from that muscle. They use it to attack and drag large animals such as moose. The bears can be super speedy, too. Over short distances, a grizzly can run faster than a horse to catch prey.

Grizzlies eat meat such as deer and fish. But their diet also includes plants and berries. These animals are called omnivores.

A grizzly has powerful paws and long, sharp claws.

A Goliath bird-eating spider crawls through a forest in South America.

This huge, hairy tarantula is a Goliath bird-eating spider. It is the largest spider in the world. The Goliath is the size of a small pizza and can overpower mice and birds. It does not spin a web, though. The spider uses its long fangs to inject deadly **venom** into its prey.

This trap-door spider is a clever predator. It makes a hole in the ground and covers it with a web. Then the spider waits in its hideout. When an insect comes by, the spider leaps out and snatches its prey.

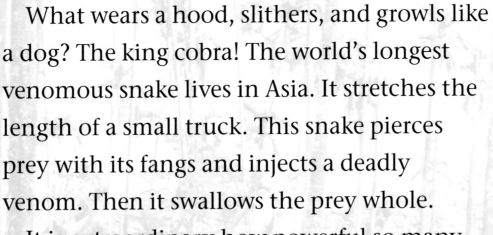

What wears a hood, slithers, and growls like a dog? The king cobra! The world's longest venomous snake lives in Asia. It stretches the length of a small truck. This snake pierces prey with its fangs and injects a deadly venom. Then it swallows the prey whole.

It is extraordinary how powerful so many predators are!

caiman   anaconda

Not all snakes poison their prey. An anaconda squeezes its prey, a caiman, to death (pictured). The anaconda is the world's largest snake. And it has a big mouth, too! The anaconda can open its mouth wide enough to swallow the entire caiman!

A king cobra can expand its hood to appear larger.

hood

Which IS More Extraordinary?

Champion Boxer

Mantis Shrimp

- This lightning-fast shrimp is like a boxer. It knocks out prey with one powerful punch of its claws.

- Its claws strike 50 times faster than you can blink your eyes.

- The shrimp's punch is so strong it can shatter a clam's shell. It can even break thick aquarium glass.

You Decide!

Get to know two powerful predators and make your own choice.

Archerfish

- An archerfish shoots a powerful jet of water from its mouth to knock prey from above into the water.

- This fish almost always hits its target—like a tasty insect on a leaf.

- The missile-like water jet can reach nearly 7 feet (2 meters) in the air.

Precision Shooter

What's for Dinner?

These fierce predators are hungry. Read the clues below and guess what each might devour for dinner.

1 An assassin bug waits on a flower for its meal to buzz by.

A kangaroo

2 The leopard seal—one of Antarctica's top predators—gobbles up this seabird.

B wasp

3 Australia's Tasmanian devil tears its teeth into this leggy leaper.

C king penguin

30

Glossary

food chain (food **chayn**):
An ordered arrangement of
animals and plants in which
each one feeds on the one
below it in the chain.

predator (**pred**-uh-tur):
An animal that hunts other
animals for food.

prey (**pray**):
Animals that are hunted
for food.

venom (**ven**-uhm):
Poison produced by some
snakes, spiders, and jellyfish.

Index

Facts for Now

Visit this Scholastic Web site for more information
on powerful predators:
www.factsfornow.scholastic.com
Enter the keywords **Powerful Predators**

About the Author

Lisa M. Herrington has written many children's books about animals.
She loves to learn fascinating facts about them. Lisa lives in Connecticut
with her husband, Ryan, and daughter, Caroline.